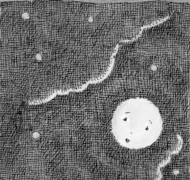

For Amelia
with our love.
S.H. & H.C.

First U.S. Edition 1992

First published in 1991 by Walker Books Ltd., London

ISBN 0-316-35250-0
Library of Congress Catalog Card Number 91-52589
Library of Congress Cataloging-in-Publication
information is available.

Joy Street Books are published by Little, Brown and Company (Inc.)

10 9 8 7 6 5 4 3 2 1

Printed and bound in Hong Kong by the
South China Printing Company (1988) Ltd.

THIS IS THE
BEAR
AND THE
SCARY NIGHT

WRITTEN BY
Sarah Hayes

ILLUSTRATED BY
Helen Craig

Little, Brown and Company
Boston   Toronto   London

This is the boy
who forgot his bear

and left him behind
in the park on a chair.

This is the bear
who looked at the moon

and hoped the boy
would come back soon.

This is the bear
alone in the park.

I'm not scared.

And these are the eyes
that glowed in the dark.

WHOOOOOOOOOOOOOO!

This is the owl
who swooped down in the
night and gave the bear
a terrible fright.

This is the bear
up in the sky.
This is the owl
who struggled to fly.

These are the claws
that couldn't hold on.
And this is the bear
who fell . . .

This is the bear
who floated all night.

This is the dark
that turned into light.

This is the man
with the slide trombone

who rescued the bear
and took him home.

This is the bear
in a warm blue sweater
who made a friend
and felt much better.

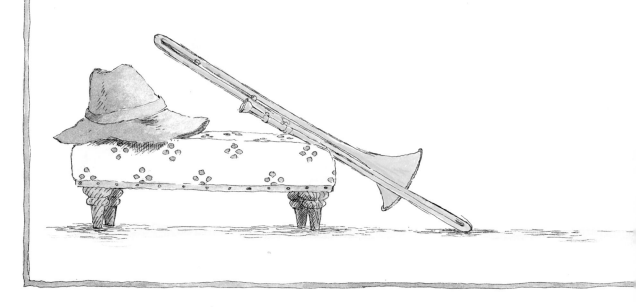

This is the boy
who remembered his bear

and ran to the park
and found him there.

This is the bear
who started to tell

how he flew through the air
and how he fell . . .

and how he floated
and how he was saved
and how he was
terribly, terribly brave.
And this is the boy
who grinned and said,
"I know a bear
who is ready for bed."

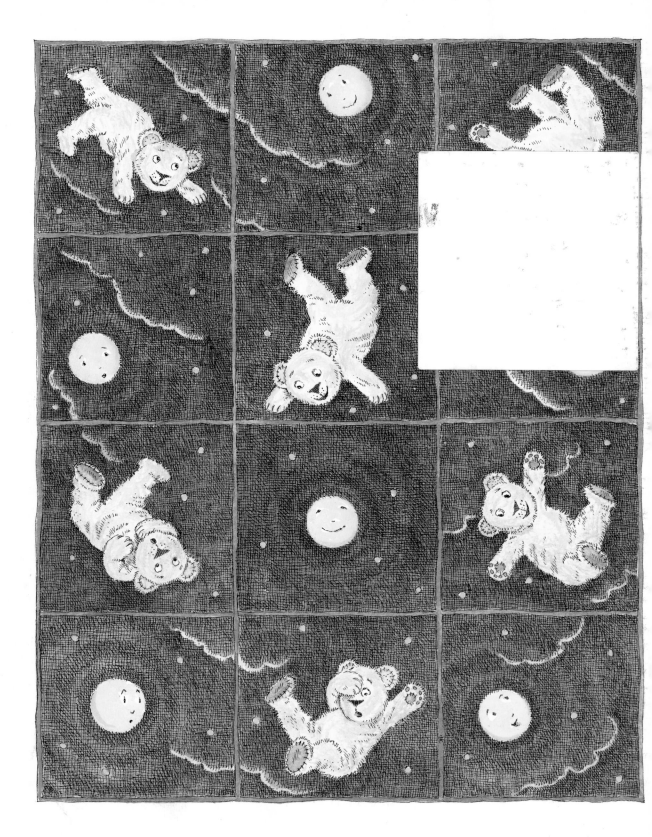